Even a little rain can paint the sky
and save a garden.

The Wind and Little Cloud, 1st Edition.

Copyright © 2006 by Susan G. Hancock. Printed and bound in the United States of America. All rights reserved. No part of this book may be reproduced or transmitted in any form or by any means, electronic or mechanical, including photocopying, recording, or by an information storage and retrieval system.

ISBN 0-9741743-0-0
LCCN 2005909425

Published by Perlycross Publishers, 2711 Centerville Road, Suite 120, PMB 5544, Wilmington, Delaware 19808.

Susan G. Hancock, Author
Robert Simmons, Illustrator
Bryce D. Gibby, Editor

PERLYCROSS PUBLISHERS
Wilmington, Delaware

"The Perle, as it flows on the north of the Churchyard, the bridge two or three hundred yards below, the vale, and the hills which shape it, are comprised in the parish of Perlycross."

R. D. Blackmore

To Dallin,
who always has time
to hear Grandma's stories.
S.H.

To Ryan, Shauna,
Chelsea and Jeff.
R.S.

The Wind and Little Cloud

By
Susan G. Hancock

Illustrated by
Robert Simmons

The Wind and Little Cloud were friends. All day every day they chased each other across the sky trying to be first to reach the white-capped mountains.

Together they sped over raging seas, across great cities, and deep jungles. They even billowed and blew their way above vast deserts.

Little Cloud never noticed the scenery below, for there were sky races going on.

The Wind always seemed to win, because he could blow here and reach there. Yet even though the Wind was faster, Little Cloud secretly considered himself to be the most important, for he could be seen while the Wind could only be felt.

Still the Wind and Little Cloud were friends.

One summer morning, as the sun was just waking up, Little Cloud looked down upon an emerald countryside.

"Oh!" he said, "We've never been here before!"

Below him rolled hills and a valley that stretched green on and on to a glistening silver lake. A tree-lined lane meandered alongside a whispering stream.

Little Cloud could see a farmhouse tucked into a flowered hillside of vegetable gardens and fruit trees.

And yes, there were meadows of buttercups and lazy cows. There was so much to see in this delicious looking place.

"Who lives in that happy house?" he wondered. Then a new feeling – almost a longing – came over Little Cloud.

"Oh my, this must be what coming home feels like."

As the Wind began his morning blow, Little Cloud felt himself gliding away from the valley that felt like home.

"STOP!" he shouted. "I do not want to play. I cannot move from this place for I don't believe I can be happy anywhere else in this wide world."

The surprised Wind whispered, "But Little Cloud, look ahead. We do more than play. Today we fly to the mystic marshlands. We are here because the plains and swamps, the hills and valleys need us. Come on, let's go!"

"I found my new home. I will not leave. No. No. No." Little Cloud was as firm as a wispy cloud could be.

The Wind paused, "I suppose I can stay for a day or two."

"I don't want that either, said Little Cloud. "For wherever you are, it blows and blows. You would disturb my peaceful valley."

"Is this what you want? Are you sure?" whistled the Wind as he skated toward the horizon.

Just to be polite Little Cloud called, "You may visit me next year or sometime after that." But the Wind was already gone.

Little Cloud stretched in the warm sunshine. He was glad to be alone and he wanted to look for lambs in the far meadow. The air was heavy, without even the slightest breeze. Little Cloud tried leaning toward the back pasture but he did not float. In fact, he could not move at all.

So he contented himself by watching three magnificent horses canter toward the brook. He looked down on them with great interest. Each drank and then slowly walked to a spot of shade beneath the cottonwoods. The morning was becoming rather hot.

The farmer and his family looked as tiny as ants to Little Cloud as he saw them working together in their gardens and fields far below. Some were picking fruit from the trees and carrying it to the barn in baskets; others were feeding livestock and gathering eggs.

As nothing covered the sun, and since the air did not stir, the day grew hotter and hotter. After a while the family went indoors. Now nothing moved, not even the aspen leaves. Little Cloud grew drowsy. "I need to sleep...sle-e-e-e-p....z z z z z."

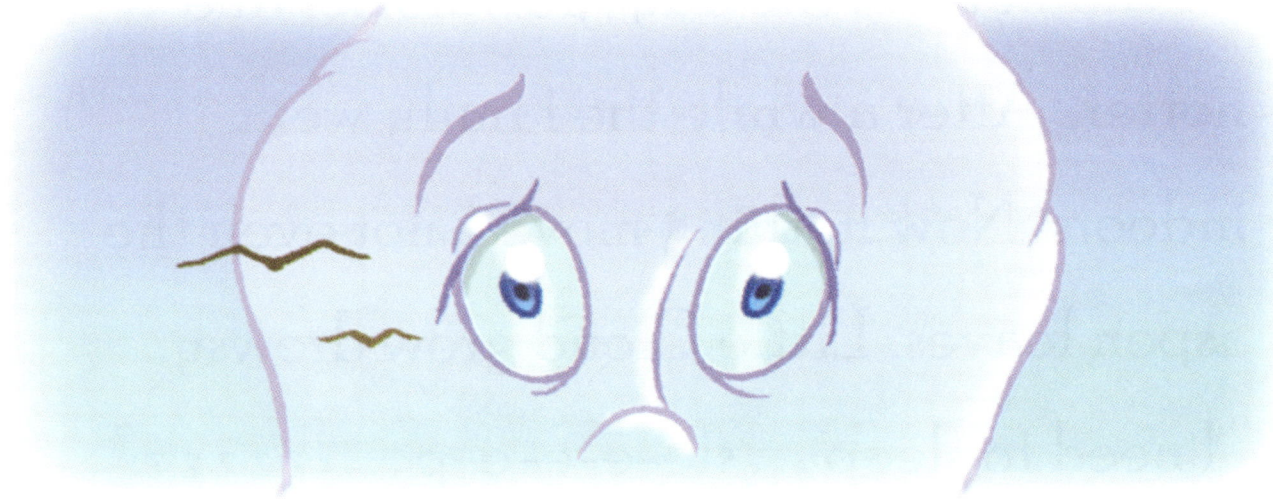

Suddenly Little Cloud roused himself. Something dreadful was happening to him.

"I am getting smaller!" he gasped, "Why this morning I was a beefy cumulus, but now I look like a washed out cirrus!" Little Cloud was horrified. He wanted to cry, but could not spare the moisture.

It was then that Little Cloud realized the Wind had been his truest friend all along.

"He faithfully gathered my vapor so I could grow. Now in this heat, I am e-v-a-p-o-r-a-t-i-n-g!" He tried calling, "Save me!" But Little Cloud was shrinking so fast his voice was only a weak whisper.

Little Cloud remembered all the days and nights he and the Wind had roamed the skies together.

He thought of the many lessons he had learned from his friend. "Look both ways before crossing a storm."

"Even a little rain can paint the sky and save a garden."

Little Cloud sighed, "He even taught me how to count the stars. And I sent Him away. Why did I think I was moving by my power? It was all Him. On my own I'm not so much as mist."

The sun beat down upon the stream.

The sun beat down upon the fields.

The sun beat down upon the orchards and gardens.

Little Cloud had become a tiny speck of vapor, just about the size of a tear.

"Good-bye, my friend," he breathed.

At that very moment the Wind tore back across the sky calling, "The marsh is not mystic without you."

Seeing how shockingly tiny Little Cloud had become, the Wind worked feverishly. He whipped moisture from above the stream and blew it into soft billows.

Before long, Little Cloud became just that – a fluffy little cloud.

"Ohhh, thank you!" sang Little Cloud, skipping with joy.

The Wind answered, "Little Cloud, this green valley feels like home…

because it IS home, and so is every hill and mountain. For all that is green is fed by you.

"You mean by US," said Little Cloud....
"Oh my, look ahead!"

And they hurried on together.